THIS BOOK

BELONGS TO:

......................................................

......................................................

THE TALE OF

*Timmy Tiptoes*

# The Tale of
# Timmy Tiptoes

BY

BEATRIX POTTER

A PETER RABBIT™
*110th Anniversary Edition*

FREDERICK WARNE

FOR MANY UNKNOWN LITTLE
FRIENDS, INCLUDING MONICA

FREDERICK WARNE

Published by the Penguin Group
Penguin Books Ltd., 80 Strand, London WC2R oRL, England
Penguin Group (USA) Inc., 375 Hudson Street, New York, New York 10014, USA
Penguin Group (Australia), 250 Camberwell Road, Camberwell,
Victoria 3124, Australia (a division of Pearson Australia Group Pty. Ltd.)
Penguin Group (Canada), 90 Eglinton Avenue East, Suite 700, Toronto,
Ontario M4P 2Y3, Canada (a division of Pearson Penguin Canada Inc.)
Penguin Books India Pvt. Ltd., 11 Community Centre, Panchsheel Park, New Delhi—110 017, In
Penguin Group (NZ), 67 Apollo Drive, Rosedale, Auckland 0632,
New Zealand (a division of Pearson New Zealand Ltd.)
Penguin Books (South Africa) (Pty.) Ltd, 24 Sturdee Avenue, Rosebank, Johannesburg 2196, South Afr

Penguin Books Ltd., Registered Offices: 80 Strand, London WC2R oRL, England

Website: www.peterrabbit.com

First published by Frederick Warne in 1911
First published with reset text and new reproductions
of Beatrix Potter's illustrations in 2002
This edition published in 2011

003 - 10 9 8 7 6 5 4 3

New reproductions copyright © Frederick Warne & Co., 2002
Original copyright in text and illustrations © Frederick Warne & Co., 1911
Frederick Warne & Co. is the owner of all rights, copyrights and trademarks
in the Beatrix Potter character names and illustrations.

Colour reproduction by
EAE Creative Colour Ltd, Norwich
Printed and bound in China

## PUBLISHER'S NOTE

By 1911, Beatrix Potter was internationally popular, and her fans included a large contingent of North American readers. To please them, she devised *The Tale of Timmy Tiptoes*, a story featuring chipmunks and grey squirrels.

In doing so, she presented herself with rather a puzzle – how to draw from life creatures which she had never seen in the wild? She appears to have relied on photographs and zoo animals, which prompted some embarrassed criticism from her publisher Harold Warne. 'There is no doubt the animals strongly resemble rabbits,' Beatrix insisted, in defence of her chipmunk illustrations. Nevertheless, Beatrix willingly made alterations, and in due course the book was published to popular and commercial success.

ONCE UPON A TIME there was a little fat comfortable grey squirrel, called Timmy Tiptoes. He had a nest thatched with leaves in the top of a tall tree; and he had a little squirrel wife called Goody.

TIMMY TIPTOES sat out, enjoying the breeze; he whisked his tail and chuckled — "Little wife Goody, the nuts are ripe; we must lay up a store for winter and spring." Goody Tiptoes was busy pushing moss under the thatch — "The nest is so snug, we shall be sound asleep all winter." "Then we shall wake up all the thinner, when there is nothing to eat in spring-time," replied prudent Timothy.

WHEN Timmy and Goody Tiptoes came to the nut thicket, they found other squirrels were there already.

Timmy took off his jacket and hung it on a twig; they worked away quietly by themselves.

Every day they made several journeys and picked quantities of nuts. They carried them away in bags, and stored them in several hollow stumps near the tree where they had built their nest.

WHEN these stumps were full, they began to empty the bags into a hole high up a tree, that had belonged to a wood-pecker; the nuts rattled down — down — down inside.

"How shall you ever get them out again? It is like a money-box!" said Goody.

"I shall be much thinner before spring-time, my love," said Timmy Tiptoes, peeping into the hole.

THEY did collect quantities — because they did not lose them! Squirrels who bury their nuts in the ground lose more than half, because they cannot remember the place.

The most forgetful squirrel in the wood was called Silvertail. He began to dig, and he could not remember. And then he dug again and found some nuts that did not belong to him; and there was a fight. And other squirrels began to dig — the whole wood was in commotion!

UNFORTUNATELY, just at this time a flock of little birds flew by, from bush to bush, searching for green caterpillars and spiders. There were several sorts of little birds, twittering different songs.

The first one sang — "Who's bin digging-up *my* nuts? Who's-been-digging-up *my* nuts?"

And another sang — "Little bit-a-bread and-*no*-cheese! Little bit-a-bread an'-*no*-cheese!"

THE squirrels followed and listened. The first little bird flew into the bush where Timmy and Goody Tiptoes were quietly tying up their bags, and it sang — "Who's-bin digging-up *my* nuts? Who's been digging-up *my*-nuts?"

Timmy Tiptoes went on with his work without replying; indeed, the little bird did not expect an answer. It was only singing its natural song, and it meant nothing at all.

BUT when the other squirrels heard that song, they rushed upon Timmy Tiptoes and cuffed and scratched him, and upset his bag of nuts. The innocent little bird which had caused all the mischief, flew away in a fright!

Timmy rolled over and over, and then turned tail and fled towards his nest, followed by a crowd of squirrels shouting — "Who's-been digging-up *my*-nuts?"

THEY caught him and dragged him up the very same tree, where there was the little round hole, and they pushed him in. The hole was much too small for Timmy Tiptoes' figure. They squeezed him dreadfully, it was a wonder they did not break his ribs. "We will leave him here till he confesses," said Silvertail Squirrel, and he shouted into the hole—

"Who's-been-digging-up *my*-nuts?"

TIMMY TIPTOES made no reply; he had tumbled down inside the tree, upon half a peck of nuts belonging to himself. He lay quite stunned and still.

GOODY TIPTOES picked up the nut bags and went home. She made a cup of tea for Timmy; but he didn't come and didn't come.

Goody Tiptoes passed a lonely and unhappy night. Next morning she ventured back to the nut-bushes to look for him; but the other unkind squirrels drove her away.

She wandered all over the wood, calling —

"Timmy Tiptoes! Timmy Tiptoes! Oh, where is Timmy Tiptoes?"

IN the meantime Timmy Tiptoes
came to his senses. He found
himself tucked up in a little moss
bed, very much in the dark,
feeling sore; it seemed to be under
ground. Timmy coughed and
groaned, because his ribs hurted
him. There was a chirpy noise,
and a small striped Chipmunk
appeared with a night light, and
hoped he felt better?

It was most kind to Timmy
Tiptoes; it lent him its night-
cap; and the house was full of
provisions.

THE Chipmunk explained that it had rained nuts through the top of the tree — "Besides, I found a few buried!" It laughed and chuckled when it heard Timmy's story. While Timmy was confined to bed, it 'ticed him to eat quantities — "But how shall I ever get out through that hole unless I thin myself? My wife will be anxious!" "Just another nut — or two nuts; let me crack them for you," said the Chipmunk. Timmy Tiptoes grew fatter and fatter!

Now Goody Tiptoes had set to work again by herself. She did not put any more nuts into the woodpecker's hole, because she had always doubted how they could be got out again. She hid them under a tree root; they rattled down, down, down. Once when Goody emptied an extra big bagful, there was a decided squeak; and next time Goody brought another bagful, a little striped Chipmunk scrambled out in a hurry.

"I⫟ is getting perfectly full-up downstairs; the sitting-room is full, and they are rolling along the passage; and my husband, Chippy Hackee, has run away and left me. What is the explanation of these showers of nuts?"

"I am sure I beg your pardon; I did not know that anybody lived here," said Mrs. Goody Tiptoes; "but where is Chippy Hackee? My husband, Timmy Tiptoes, has run away too." "I know where Chippy is; a little bird told me," said Mrs. Chippy Hackee.

SHE led the way to the wood-pecker's tree, and they listened at the hole.

Down below there was a noise of nut crackers, and a fat squirrel voice and a thin squirrel voice were singing together —

"My little old man and I fell out,
　How shall we bring this matter about?
　Bring it about as well as you can,
　And get you gone, you little old man!"

"You could squeeze in, through that little round hole," said Goody Tiptoes. "Yes, I could," said the Chipmunk, "but my husband, Chippy Hackee, bites!"

Down below there was a noise of cracking nuts and nibbling; and then the fat squirrel voice and the thin squirrel voice sang—

"For the diddlum day
    Day diddle dum di!
    Day diddle diddle dum day!"

THEN Goody peeped in at the hole, and called down — "Timmy Tiptoes! Oh fie, Timmy Tiptoes!" And Timmy replied, "Is that you, Goody Tiptoes? Why, certainly!"

He came up and kissed Goody through the hole; but he was so fat that he could not get out.

Chippy Hackee was not too fat, but he did not want to come; he stayed down below and chuckled.

AND so it went on for a fortnight; till a big wind blew off the top of the tree, and opened up the hole and let in the rain.

Then Timmy Tiptoes came out, and went home with an umbrella.

But Chippy Hackee continued to camp out for another week, although it was uncomfortable.

AT last a large bear came walking through the wood. Perhaps he also was looking for nuts; he seemed to be sniffing around.

CHIPPY HACKEE went home in
a hurry!

AND when Chippy Hackee got home, he found he had caught a cold in his head; and he was more uncomfortable still.

AND now Timmy and Goody Tiptoes keep their nut-store fastened up with a little padlock.

AND whenever that little bird sees the Chipmunks, he sings — "Who's-been-digging-up *my*-nuts? Who's been digging-up *my*-nuts?" But nobody ever answers!

THE END